Little Bunny's Cool Tool Set

Maribeth Boelts

Illustrated by Kathy Parkinson

Albert Whitman & Company • Morton Grove, Illinois

✳————————————————————————————————

Library of Congress Cataloging-in-Publication Data

Boelts, Maribeth, 1964-
    Little Bunny's cool tool set / written by Maribeth Boelts;
illustrated by Kathy Parkinson.
        p.   cm.
Summary: Little Bunny usually shares, but when he takes his new
tool set to preschool for show-and-tell, he doesn't even want his
best friend to use it.
    ISBN 0-8075-4584-8
    [1. Tools—Fiction. 2. Sharing—Fiction. 3. Friendship—Fiction.
    4. Rabbits—Fiction.] I. Parkinson, Kathy, ill. II. Title.
PZ7.B635744Lg 1997   96-54862
[E]--dc21   CIP
                                                    AC

Designed by Karen A. Yops.
The text of this book is set in Benguiat Gothic.
The illustrations are rendered in watercolor and ink.

TO
HEATHER, JOSH,
HANNAH AND SARAH,
AND TO # WILLIAM
WHO IS LEARNING TO SHARE!

——————————— MB

TO
DAVID AND LAURA
WITH WHOM WE'D LIKE TO SHARE MORE TIME!

KP

Little Bunny shook his bank as he walked to the hardware store with Papa.

"Are you sure I have enough money, Papa?" he asked.

Papa smiled. "I'm sure, LB. You've saved your money for a very long time."

"Look at this, Papa!" LB said. "It has a real hammer and a screwdriver and nails and a big belt to put all the tools in!"

When they left the hardware store, Papa carried the empty bank and LB carried a brand-new tool set.

Patrick was waiting in the driveway when they returned home.

"Did you get your tool set?" Patrick asked.

LB pulled the bag close. "Yes."

"Want to build something?"

"Not right now," LB said. "Maybe later."

All afternoon LB played with his tool set—sawing,

hammering,

unscrewing,

and measuring.

At bedtime Mama said, "Tomorrow is a preschool day, LB. Were you going to bring something for show and tell?"

LB pulled the tool set out from under his blanket.

"Are you sure?" Mama asked. "Sharing can be hard with something brand-new."

"Not for me, Mama," LB promised. "I always share."

At preschool, LB wiggled while he waited for his turn to show and tell.

Mitzie brought a big yellow leaf, and she passed it around.

Sam brought a picture of his new baby sister, and he passed it around.

Eleanor brought a coin from a different country, and she passed it around.

Finally, it was LB's turn. "This is my tool set!" he exclaimed, in a voice that was not an inside voice. "I bought it with my own money. It has a hammer and a measuring tape and a screwdriver and a real belt that you wear when you do your work."

"It's very nice," said Miss Violet. "Would you like to pass it around?"

LB looked at his new tool set, and then he looked at all the children.

"Um. . .I don't think so," he said. "They might break it or lose the nails, or maybe they might get hurt or something."

"I understand," said Miss Violet.

When show and tell was over, it was free time.

"Do you want to play?" asked Patrick.

LB frowned. "I'm kinda busy again."

"Can I see your tool set?"

"You can see it, but you better not touch it."

Seeing it was okay for a little while, but then Patrick's
hand reached out to touch the measuring tape.

"You're not supposed to touch it!" LB said.

"Then can I look at that thing with the bubble?"

"It's called a level, and no—you can't look at it."

"You're mean."

"Am not."

While LB was putting all the tools back in the box, Patrick picked up the level.

"Give that back, Patrick!"

Patrick held it up over LB's head. "I just want to see how it works."

LB jumped up to grab it, but Patrick was taller.
So instead of jumping again, LB gave Patrick a hard
p-u-s-h, and Patrick and the level fell to the ground.

Patrick began to cry. Loudly.

"Patrick!" said Miss Violet. "Are you all right?"

Patrick sniffed. "LB pushed me and he wouldn't let me touch his dumb tool set and he's not my friend anymore."

"LB," said Miss Violet, "Did you push Patrick?"

LB nodded and swallowed. He thought that maybe he was getting a sore throat.

"You'll need to sit down at the table and think for a while, Little Bunny," Miss Violet said firmly. "We don't push in preschool."

LB sat in the chair. At first he was mad.

Then he was sad.

And then he was. . .sorry.

Miss Violet knelt down on the floor next to LB.
"I know it's hard to share things that are very
special to us, LB, but it was wrong to push Patrick.
He could have really gotten hurt."

"Maybe I can say 'sorry' to Patrick?"

"That would be a very good thing to do."

Patrick was eating his snack.

"Sorry," said LB.

Patrick drank the last of his milk very s-l-o-w-l-y. Finally, he looked at LB and wiped his mouth on his sleeve. "Okay," he said.

LB and Patrick ate all of LB's apple slices and made plans to build the greatest hideout ever.

"I'll share my wood and my brownies and my grape juice," said LB.

"My dad gave me some paint that you just have to mix with water. I can bring that," Patrick added. "And can I use that thing with the bubble?"

"Well. . ." LB thought for a moment. "You can play with the hammer."

"Okay," Patrick agreed.

On Saturday, Patrick came over with his paint and paintbrush.

"I'll paint while you hammer," he told LB.

Patrick painted. LB hammered. Then LB painted and Patrick hammered.

"I like hammering better than painting," said Patrick.

"You do?" LB said.

"But guess what else, LB? I'm going to save all my money so I can buy my own tool set. Then I'll have my own hammer."

"Good idea," said LB, as he dipped his brush in the paint. "But you can just use mine until you do."